THE CORT CHRONICLES BOOK 3

# Rebirth

# David D. Bernstein

ILLUSTRATED BY VICTOR AGUILAR

outskirts
press

Outskirts Press, Inc.
http://www.outskirtspress.com

Paperback ISBN: 978-1-9772-3842-9
Hardback ISBN: 978-1-9772-3843-6

Library of Congress Control Number: 2021900094

Illustrations by: Victor Guiza.
Illustrations © 2021 Outskirts Press, Inc. All rights reserved - used with permission.

Outskirts Press and the "OP" logo are trademarks belonging to Outskirts Press, Inc.

PRINTED IN THE UNITED STATES OF AMERICA

# Dedication

I want to dedicate this book to my grandmother Nina, who always kept things in order. She was a wonderful wife, mother, and grandmother. She kept fighting till her last breath. We love her very much and we will miss her greatly, but memories of her will be with us forever.

*A strong woman full of love.*
April 29, 1923 to March 30, 2020

# Table of Contents

# Chapter 1
# Supermarket

"**W**hat happened here?" Andy asked.

"When I left, it was empty," Zack replied, pointing to the supermarket in front of them.

"Are you sure?" Wendy asked.

"I am positive. Something is wrong here."

They watched as people of different sizes walked in and out. Each one was carrying a familiar square box—the same ones Andy and Zack saw everywhere in the future.

"I thought we destroyed them recently," Andy said.

"We are not in Trinity anymore, little bro," Zack said.

"I think we are." Andy pointed to a sign in front of them: it read Trinity, NY.

"That was not there when I left," Zack said.

"Maybe it was put up during those four missing hours," Andy said.

"That is impossible. A sign takes years to plan and raise money for."

"You are right. How weird."

"It might be best if we went to the store; we might get some answers," Wendy said.

"Good idea Wendy." Zack said as he took her hand in his.

Andy noticed a large smile appear on Wendy's face.

They both walked forward, not even looking back for a minute at Andy. Andy frowned as he followed.

Entering the store was a big surprise for everyone; it had been closed for three years. Inside they found several aisles full of food. It had everything an individual needed. It kind of reminded them of a massive Walmart. There were three floors full of goods. Many of the products were CORT brand, but most of them were normal goods found in any large supermarket.

Wendy approached a clerk, and asked, "Excuse me, sir, how long has this store been here?"

"You must be new in town; we have been here thirteen years now," he said.

"Thank you," Wendy said.

"Are you looking for anything in particular?"

"Just looking around. Thanks again." Wendy walked back to the boys. "They have been here thirteen years," she said.

"Wow, that is older than I am," Andy said.

"Let's look around a bit," Zack suggested.

Inside was like a maze. The party even noticed golf carts moving around carrying goods and people.

"I have never seen a store like this one," Zack admitted.

"It is so cool," Andy added.

"We must be aware of all our surroundings," Wendy said.

"What can we do without any magic or weapons?" Andy said.

"I highly doubt anyone will attack us; it is a store, not a war zone," Zack said.

"I agree, we came from a war zone, but here seems to be very peaceful and quiet," Wendy said.

The children continued to walk around, looking for something they could buy. Strangely enough there seemed to be no weapons for sale, only other goods.

"It is too quiet in my view," Andy said.

"We will be very observant, just in case," Zack said as he took Wendy's hand again.

"I learned not to trust silence," Wendy said.

"We should be on guard," Andy added.

They tiptoed in the hallways; huge shelves of goods were everywhere. If only Andy could remember his flying ability he learned of in the future. He could not understand how some of the goods could not be reached by a person—maybe by a giant. That thought gave him chills. Could this new world have monsters in it?

The party started to move even quieter now, looking in all directions. They saw many goods; some they did not even recognize. The products were a mix of tech, food, and other goods. Andy thought back to the last time he remembered that store open. Back it only sold food. It also was not as massive. The store was now the size of 100 football fields and had three floors in it. The items were piled from wall to wall. Goods filled every bit of space except the hallways, which were clean and open so customers could move around freely. It was amazing what could be found here.

"Do you think we could buy weapons somewhere here?" Wendy asked.

"I truly doubt it, honey," Zack said. He took out a paper and showed it to her and Andy.

"Three years ago, a massive shooting took place that killed a thousand people in one night. It caused Washington, DC to ban all weapons and overwrite the Second Amendment. Since that time our country has become a more peaceful nation."

"Hold on a minute...where did you find this?" Andy pointed at the paper.

"Little bro, it was in the book section of the store."

"When did you get to stop by there?" Andy asked.

"We passed by it just ten minutes ago," Zack said. "I thought it would not hurt to learn a bit of history of the new planet."

"Did you learn anything else, Zack?" Wendy asked with concern. The moment she said it three darts just missed the party's heads.

"I thought weapons were banned!" Andy screamed.

"It means there must be a black market for them somewhere," Wendy said as three more darts missed them again.

"Let's run now and take the book with you," Andy called out.

The party took off fast, running back to the place they entered. Darts were flying everywhere damaging all kinds of goods melted as they were hit.

"It looks like we must be wanted criminals," Zack said.

"It is not funny, bro," Andy added.

After ten minutes of running, they found themselves outside the store. Something very strange was going on this new Earth. They had to know what it was.

After catching their breath just outside the store, the three of them sat on a bench not too far away. They finally found peace again.

"What was that about?" Wendy asked.

"I am almost certain we are wanted criminals," Andy implied.

"How could that be?" Wendy asked.

"We must have done something in the future to change the past," Zack suggested.

"How is that possible? The future did not even happen yet," Andy said.

"I have a feeling time really does not exist," Zack said.

"It's possible," Wendy added.

It reminded Andy of the dark world he had been in; it was there that time had no meaning.

"Guys, I have a feeling what has happened here is my fault," he said.

"Why do you say that?" Zack asked.

"It all started back in your home world Wendy. To save one of the sages, I had to enter dark world, and it was there that Zoey vanished. I believe that what we see in the present was caused by that event."

"You know how dangerous the dark world is," Wendy said.

"I certainly do, I think that dark world has appeared

here on our earth and changed everything that we loved," Andy said.

"Oh, little brother, what will I do with you?" Zack said.

"I think it might be best for us to get home; it may be the only place that is safe now," Andy suggested.

"No, the dark world likes to be in one area: It is not in a whole world, but only part of one," Wendy said.

It made lots of sense to Andy. He remembered being in one area when he visited dark world.

"It only appears where it is safe. I have a feeling dark world is only underground or on CORT territory," Wendy said. It made sense to them; that supermarket was CORT territory, and they were attacked only there, not outside.

"Let's check out our house, and read more from this book," Zack showed everyone a large book with the title *Laws of this Land*.

"That might give us many answers," Wendy added.

"Let's go!" Andy went forward.

# Chapter 2
# Home

**S**trangely enough, most of the streets had remained the same, and the trio found the home easily. It was when they got closer that they noticed it was empty. The front door was wide open, and when they entered, the table was set up for a meal. It was like something happened fast.

Their parents were just taken by someone. There was scattered furniture and garbage in the living room, and it smelled like fresh dirt.

"Mom, Dad, Buddy?" Andy called out. There was no answer. There seemed to be signs of struggle everywhere. Blood stains covered the walls, and, in a few areas, the familiar gray dust covered the floor.

Zack understood, CORT was still alive and active here. All the work he, Wendy, John, and his brother had done meant nothing now. At least he had the two people he loved most next to him. They would have to work together to save their planet too. Zack hoped the book he picked up would give them some answers.

"Let's check the house out," Wendy suggested.

"Good idea, Wendy," Andy said.

After a full house sweep, they found it was empty. *What has happened to this world?* Andy wondered. How could they do anything without weapons or skills? It would have been much easier for them earlier.

The party moved to the basement,
and they saw them: six circles
attached drawn in red on the wall.

It made lots of sense after all they had been through. I guess nothing came easy for them.

Wendy locked the front door. It amazed the children that the bathrooms still worked in the house. While searching the home Andy found some strange markings on the walls; deep in his subconscious mind he thought it was magic protecting them. He couldn't explain why his dog and parents were missing.

The kids did find a large meat loaf in the oven, perfectly browned. This would be a treat for them; it had been so long since they had enjoyed Mom's cooking.

Near the meat loaf Zack found a short, scribbled note: "Dear darlings, our magic protection has been cracked somehow. You must fix it to be safe again." It ended with a picture of a sign and was stained in blood.

"Why does your mom mention magic?" Wendy asked.

"I have no idea. We never had magic in this world," Zack said.

"It is very odd, isn't it," Andy was puzzled.

"Let's look around the house more," Zack suggested.

"I noticed some drawings in the basement," Andy said.

"That might be it," Wendy said.

"Let's hurry downstairs," Zack said.

"Do not forget the letter," Wendy said.

"I have it." Andy waved it in the air.

The party moved to the basement, and there they

saw them: six circles, attached, drawn in red on the wall. Three of them had strange writing on them and the others did not.

Looking at the letter in his hands, Andy saw more writing that seemed to fit into the other circles. "Do you think this is it?" Andy pointed at the wall.

"It is worth a try; the pictures seem to match," Wendy said.

Andy looked around the basement and saw a red pen just a few feet away.

"Grab that for me, Zack," Andy said.

Zack walked over and brought the pen back to his brother.

"You are the sage here," Wendy said.

Andy took a few deep breaths and closed his eyes; a distant hot feeling came to his body. He still had a spark of magic inside him. The image on the paper started floating above his head. Shapes changed and writings moved around. They formed brand-new words. After opening his eyes, Andy filled in the empty circles on the wall with them.

After he was done the whole basement lit up in golden light that moved up and covered the whole house.

"Amazing, little brother, you still have it in you," Zack said.

Andy smiled at his brother and went upstairs. Once again, the protection magic came back. It meant two things for Andy: he still had magic left and they had a safe zone now.

Soon, everyone was sitting at the kitchen table and eating the meat loaf. It had been a while since they had a good meal.

"What do we do now?" Wendy asked.

"I guess we will read the book." Zack placed the book on the table and opened it to a list. "I think this will cover all the changes here in a nutshell." Zack said.

The main changes were no guns, no subways, and no underground activities.

The party did not understand what was going on here, but they hoped to discover for themselves.

"I think we should explore New York," Andy suggested.

"What is that?" Wendy asked.

"It is one of our largest cities," Zack said.

"It is a good place to start," Andy said.

"How can we get there, and do we have money to do so?" Wendy asked.

"I will be right back; Mom has an emergency fund," Andy stated.

"How do you know that?" Zack asked.

"I just do. Mom was always scared to tell you about it, Zack." With those words Andy disappeared. He got back five minutes later carrying a fistful of cash. "This should be enough for us," he said with a smile.

It was a huge surprise for both Zack and Wendy.

"Once again you are a life saver," Wendy said. Right before they left the house, the party felt warmth hit them. They hoped it was magic protection.

# Chapter 3
# New York

**O**utside the house a strong pull was coming from somewhere. The party was not sure what it was, but it felt very safe and comfortable for them.

"I wonder if the magic protection came with us," Wendy said.

"It does seem that way," Andy replied.

"I think it is very possible," Zack agreed.

As they walked down the street away from their home, the pull got stronger. Eventually they all adjusted, and the pull became part of them.

It was much easier to move now, and what they needed to do was find a way to get to New York City. It was a forty-minute ride.

"I wish we had that transport we used back in my home," Wendy said.

"It would be very helpful, but I believe we will need to call a cab this time," Zack said.

"Darling, what is a cab?" Wendy asked.

"It is like a car, with a driver," Zack explained.

"Okay," Wendy said, still confused by what Zack meant.

Amazingly one of the items Andy brought was a fully charged iPhone. Mom was always the kind of lady who prepared for everything under the sun. Andy remembered that she used to say, "We can never be over prepared in this world." It was her way of thinking that saved the kids.

Andy was surprised that the iPhone still existed here. It even looked the same. In general, the technology had changed a bit more than expected, but at least some classics still were around. Andy learned to use the iPhone four years ago, when he got one as a gift from his parents. He turned it on normally and thank goodness there was no password. He got into Google and searched for taxi cabs. A list of about fifteen in the area came up. One of those looked awfully familiar; it was called Trinity Cabs. He remembered they used that company a few times back in his real home. When he dialed the phone number a familiar voice answered. It was great to hear someone he knew.

"Hello, Andy," the voice said. "How are your parents?"

"They are working hard, Greg."

"Nice to hear. How can I help you, Andy?"

"We need a cab to New York."

"How will you pay for that cab?" Greg asked.

"It would be cash."

"Excellent, your mom told me that you would call for a cab, and I got her permission to get one for you," Greg said.

"Okay, it will be me, Zack, and a friend."

"I will dispatch a cab there in five minutes."

"Wonderful, take care, Greg."

"You too, young man." With those words the phone was put down.

"Mom and Dad must have vanished recently," Andy said.

"Why do you say that?" Zack asked.

"Mom gave permission for Greg to send a cab to drive us."

"It is our Greg, Dad's good friend?" Zack asked, surprised.

"Amazingly it is, just talked to him," Andy said.

"Something is way weird here," Wendy said.

"I agree. We will have all our senses ready," Zack said.

Ten minutes later a cab pulled into the driveway. In big red letters was written "Trinity Cabs," with a phone number on the back and front.

A tall man came out and held the door open for the children. They got in and off they went. They arrived at the New York Public Library in forty-five minutes with little traffic.

"This is where your mom told Greg to drop you off," the driver said.

"Thanks, sir. How much?" Andy asked.

"You got a fifty percent discount, so thirty dollars please," the driver said.

Andy smiled and handed the man forty dollars.

"Thank you, Andy, please say hello to your mom and dad for me."

"I will," Andy said.

The driver handed Andy a card with a cell phone number. "If you need me, just call."

After the children got out, the taxi drove off.

"Wow, what a deal," Zack said.

"It is something Dad would do for us," Andy said.

"Yes, in our world too," Zack said.

Soon the children entered the New York Public Library.

The brothers recognized the large ceilings and the hard stone walls. The same lions guarded the entrance, and the floor was wood. Most of the library seemed the same except one new section the kids noticed.

It was on the first floor. That section had about thirty large computers and shelves full of history books. They looked around and noticed only five open computers that did not even require library cards to access. In large black letters were the words: "Thanks to CORT Corp."

"Something is very fishy," Wendy admitted.

"I agree. Why would CORT give free computers?" Zack asked.

"It is very strange," Andy added.

"I say let's check them out. We might learn something," Wendy went over to one.

The children joined her. It was engraved in wood and had red letters that spelled "CORT."

The first thing they saw was a log-in.

"That is the catch," Zack assumed. "CORT forces you to put in your information and they can track you and arrest you if needed."

"Definitely something they would do," Wendy said.

"I say we take a look at the history books over

there; we don't need to put in detailed information," Andy said.

"Good idea, bro," Zack said.

They moved away from the computers and walked over to the bookshelves: The books were in order by year from 1990 to 2000. Nearby was a table where they were able to sit at.

"What year should we look at?" Zack asked.

"Let's look at 1992, a good place to start," Wendy suggested.

Zack took the book from the shelves and found a section on Trinity and CORT.

It read: "A falling star fell, hitting the dirt. Scientists did not know what it was. They found a large burn mark in the grass, but the item was missing. People of Trinity never solved the riddle."

"That is interesting," Wendy said.

"It seems it all started back then," Andy suggested.

"Do you think CORT was involved?" Zack asked.

"From what I learned as a resistance leader, most likely they were," Wendy said.

"Yes, they always had their nose in the bacon," Zack said.

"It must be connected to all these changes," Andy said.

"How do we get there without a time machine?" Zack asked.

"I guess we need to do more research first and solve the problem," Andy said.

"This is the best place to start," Wendy said.

The children continued to dig up what they could. People came in and out and the cycle continued. The party sat at the same table. With the three of them they were able to go through an enormous amount of history books. Before they knew it, a voice said over the loudspeaker, "Thank you all for your business, but the library has to close in thirty minutes. If you have any books to take out, please come to the front."

The voice went silent.

Zack said, "That is very odd; I do not remember a loudspeaker in our old library."

"From what I understand from the books," Wendy said, "your world had a huge technology burst in 1992, and the people were not ready."

"Yes, all seemed to take place after the thing fell from the sky," Andy said.

"I think we have learned enough, but I just have one unanswered question," Zack said. "What happened to our train and subway system?"

Suddenly, they heard a speeding train outside. The children ran out of the building, and they saw it—a track in the sky, large brick stairs engulfed in tropical plants, glowing in several colors. They climbed up.

"Wow, I guess it is our train," Wendy said.

The children could not believe they missed it on the way over. It proved the theory they just learned about.

"Should we go home?" Zack asked.

"We could find out if the train stops there," Andy said.

"That is a great idea," Zack said.

The children climbed the stairs and found an information booth just at the end of them. A lady with large spectacles looked at the children.

"How can I help you children?" she asked with a large smile.

"Miss, does the train stop in Trinity?" Wendy asked.

"Yes, young lady, it does."

"Three one-way tickets please.

"How will you pay that, cash, fingerprint, or credit?"

Wendy gave a strange look toward Zack, who just moved his head up and down.

"Cash," Wendy said.

"Okay. Fifteen dollars," the lady said.

Andy handed her a ten- and a five-dollar bill.

"Thank you, young man." She gave them three tickets. On them was written "station number 2 to 6." The tickets were like the ones Andy used in the past. "You will find your train on air tunnel two; it leaves in fifteen minutes. Thank you for riding Air Train."

The children walked past her and looked around. It looked like a regular train station with a few changes.

First, they noticed several machines with pictures of food and other stuff. Second, they saw huge plasma screens hanging everywhere. Commercials flashed at them all the time. Finally, they noticed people everywhere. It must have been rush hour.

They found air tunnel 2 easily; it was a tube with

the number 2 on it. In front, digital letters flashed: station stops: Grand Central, 125 Street, Fort Smith, the Gardens, Area 1, Area 2, Area 3, Trinity, Area 4, Section 1, Brookville, Section 2, and The End.

The children could not believe what they saw. It was a commercial and digital world combined with a plant world. The plants were scattered everywhere. They were all kind of colors and sizes. Their exotic smell was everywhere. It was so cool! Yet, one question remained, What happened to their world?

# Chapter 4
# Rebirth

**A** loud bang filled the underground, and lost voices echoed as steam arose. The banging of iron and lead was everywhere. It all started with one small chip that became an underground city. The army had to grow, and slave labor was critical. CORT had been planning to rise from the ashes once again. They had been given a second chance to become an empire. They were destroyed the first time by four simple kids, yet one mistake was made that gave the robots hope again.

Soon, the underground would open and swallow whole cities. They had been planning for twenty years. All has been done in silence. The process had started long ago. CORT had been planting agents and sending goods above ground. That place was called Earth. Lucky for them they had lots of money, and the greed inside people's hearts gave CORT allies.

They had been observing the world above closely as it fell apart. They witnessed death, war, and hatred. Each major event made them stronger. There were many people above ground who could be brainwashed and paid off with money—little green notes with numbers and pictures of dead presidents on them.

The young man ran up to Sam. "I have to call the council right away. I have major news."

A loud bang filled up the underground,
lost voices echoed as steam scattered everywhere.

"Go on, Mitch, I will pass it on to them," Sam said in its deep metallic voice.

"The kids are here," Mitch reported.

"What kids?"

"Three of the four from the video you showed us, the ones you want dead."

"Are you sure of it?" Sam yelled as all his screens flashed fast.

"Yes sir, I managed to take a photo, near the supermarket." Mitch placed the photo on a tray that Sam released.

After a quick scan, Sam's screens turned red with pictures of the three kids and a brief description.

Confirmed, Wendy, leader Old York resistance. Confirmed, Andy, super sage enemy number one, and Zack, older brother, big risk. "Thank you, Mitch. You can pick up your reward in room three, four million greens," Sam said.

"Thank you, sir," Mitch said as he left the room.

"The Center Room" flashed in red. "Emergency council meeting!" a voice yelled.

# Chapter 5
# Bubble

The train took off and the New York Public Library became a distant blur within minutes. Yet, Zack noticed something very weird as they flew by; he saw a large white bubble floating above the ancient building.

"Did you see that" Zack asked.

"See what, big bro?" Andy responded.

"A major change over the New York Public Library." Zack noticed.

"What changes Zack?"

"Our beloved building is covered by a bubble."

"How is that possible? When we were inside, it felt normal," Andy said. "Maybe it is some kind of high-tech trick, and the library really does not exist anymore."

"Little brother, from what I saw so far, nothing will surprise me one bit," Zack said.

The Trinity train stop appeared in thirty minutes; the other stops seemed like normal towns, but the question still lurked: why were most of them named after numbers? Could they be controlled by CORT? How large were they?

Many questions needed to be answered, the children knew about the situation from the research.

The Trinity station was amazing. The walls were covered with art, and beautiful tropical plants everywhere. There was much less technology around. No food machines or plasma screens. It did have a few paper commercials on the walls. One piece of art caught the party's eyes; it was a scene from the future they came from. It was a mural of Andy, John, Wendy, and Zack who were smiling from the painting. Engraved below the picture were the words "Our heroes. We will miss them."

"Do you see it?" Andy asked.

"I can't believe we were honored," Zack said.

"I have a huge question. How did this picture get here? It took place 101 years in the future," Wendy was puzzled.

"It is odd, indeed, my darling," Zack hugged Wendy and once again kissed her on the lips in front of Andy.

He would never have believed his older brother, a true nerd, would find such a pretty girlfriend. He felt unwanted, but since he loved his brother, it was okay.

"Guys, I have a theory," Andy called out.

"What is that Andy?" Wendy looked at him.

"What if the two times blended with each other and this timeline is just a myth," Andy said.

"In science anything is possible," Zack said.

"If it is the case, we must research it right away," Wendy called out, full of excitement.

"If it is true, we might be able to go back to 1992 and stop all that is coming," Zack added.

"We must get back to the library right away," Wendy said.

"I have a feeling it will be safer for us to go tomorrow," Zack suggested.

"Why is that?" Wendy asked. Zack screamed look pointing to the sky.

The party looked up and noticed a news board: It was massive and had moving red ink lines.

*"News flash: We have learned of extremely dangerous people among us; they have the power to destroy whole cities. They are armed and dangerous. Whoever brings them alive to CORT Central will be rewarded handsomely."* The lines were followed by pictures of Wendy, Zack, and Andy. *"Our most wanted."* the image stopped, and other news flashed by.

"Once again we are in a bubble," Wendy stated.

"It does not surprise me one bit," Andy said.

"What we need is to find some kind of weapons," Zack said.

"From all we studied and read, I have a feeling that it will be impossible," Wendy said.

"The other problem is we do not have any connections like you did back home," Zack said.

"We do not have any more money either," Andy added. "One more thing—we are children, and no one will sell weapons to us."

"Great point, little bro."

"All we can do now is watch our backs and make sure no one recognizes us."

"Time for a makeover," Wendy decided.

"What do you have in mind?" Zack wondered.

"I have a few tricks up my sleeve," Wendy smiled.

"That means we have to go shopping," Zack said.

"That is dangerous. I think we might be able to find some things in our house," Andy suggested.

"First we have to get there," Zack said.

With those words, the party started moving faster, and did not look at anyone or at anything.

After they exited the station and went down a massive stairway, they found out that the station was just a ten-minute walk from their home. They walk out a few minutes north of City Center, on Main Street. They did not even expect to be so close to home.

"We should move fast; we have a ten-minute walk," Andy hurried.

Main Street was buzzing with activity, vendors were everywhere, and delicious smells filled the air. The world they were in was almost the same as their home. It had a few differences no underground subways and more advanced technology.

They found the home easily. Lucky for them they made it safely. The magic circle was once again connected.

"We have made it," Zack said.

"I guess everyone knows us now," Andy added.

"We will have to take care of that," Wendy said.

The children searched the house for new disguises and a new look. It had to be done since now they would be hunted.

# Chapter 6
# The Hunted

**W**endy found some old clothing, scissors, and some old hats. She also found a purple dress that looked like it would fit her perfectly.

She first cut her hair short, stripped all her clothing, and put on the dress. The final touch was some purple nail polish and a pair of old reading glasses.

The brothers were impressed by her work. She reminded them of a librarian or a teacher.

"Wow, what a makeover, darling," Zack praised her.

Andy was impressed as well; she would not be recognized by anyone.

"Now, boys, it is your turn to get a new look. I will make you my bodyguards," Wendy said with a smile.

"I am in your hands, my love."

"Shut your mouth and go sit in this chair. Art takes time to master."

Zack did as he was told; right away Wendy got to work on him. She gave him a new look with a haircut, and she told him to change his clothes. Zack did everything he was asked. He was madly in love with this girl.

After the work, Andy could not recognize his brother one bit. He was like a new man. He looked a little funny, but out of respect, Andy did not want to laugh. He knew he would be next in line.

"Okay, Andy, your turn now," Wendy invited him to sit on the chair.

He got in the chair. Andy also got a nice haircut, and Wendy handed him some of his dad's old clothing. It felt very weird to be in a home that was both old and new for him. "I will be back down soon." Andy grabbed the clothing and went upstairs to his room. It had pretty much stayed the same. His old science trophies were lined up on the shelves, his old wornout bike stood in the corner, and all his game systems were still connected. It felt great to be in his old room again. Even his favorite blanket was on his bed.

Andy had so much to think about. But even though he had all his stuff in this different world, he missed Buddy and his parents the most. He loved Zack very much, but with Wendy around, he was drifting away.

Andy also had deep respect for Wendy, but he felt quite different now. It was like two different worlds had melded into one. He had heard of this happening in science, but through rumors only. Now it truly was happening, and it probably was his entire fault. Guilt was eating him alive and he did not know what was to come.

Andy fell on his bed, put his head down into his pillows, and cried. He got up, stepped in front of his room mirror, and stripped all his clothing off. He was changing in so many ways and he did not know if it was for the better or worse.

His dad's clothing felt homey to him; they still had his dad's scent. Even with everything else that was happening, that remained the same. He walked downstairs, and the moment he entered the living room, he saw Zack and Wendy at it again. They were kissing. He turned away, trying to keep his feelings intact.

"Bodyguards do not kiss their boss," Andy said.

"Oh, you are back, little bro," Zack said as he moved away.

"What is our battle plan?"

"We use what we have in our grip." Wendy pointed to several items that could be deadly: iron pots, kitchen knives, and fire starters.

"Something Mom used to say, use what you got," Andy reminded his brother.

Within sixty minutes the children were ready. It was getting dark outside now, and they had to sleep before going back to the library.

The boys were happy to be back in their rooms, and Wendy decided to sleep in their parents' bedroom.

Well, anyway, they all had their own rooms for the night. It was comfortable to be on a soft bed. It seemed forever since everything had happened.

The children fell asleep to the buzzing of the magic spell that had kept them in a safe zone from the dangers outside.

While they slept, the alert spread like wildfire, and lots of people would be looking for them. They could not trust anyone except each other now.

It would be a hard journey without the gifts they had back in Wendy's world. Yet, deep inside they hoped that they could reactivate them. They would need their gifts more than ever now.

Andy had vivid dreams or locked-up memories gone by. He saw himself floating above huge groups of CORT officers and taking them out. It felt so real to him until he woke up seven hours later with the rise of the sun.

Zack had a deep sleep and could not remember anything he saw in his dream.

Wendy dreamed of her old resistance group back on her planet. She missed them very much, but from what she was seeing here in the past, most likely everyone she had known was dead or a prisoner back home. She also woke up with the rise of the sun. At first, she was confused about where she was, but in five minutes it all came back to her.

She was starting to question if she made the right choice by coming with Zack and Andy back to their home. It was her duty to help them like they helped her. She still remembered the promise she made to their grandfather, so she was in debt to his family.

It also was hard for her to believe that the place she left was the same. In a way Zack and Andy were all she had left in her life now.

After washing and dressing in the new clothing, Wendy joined the boys in the kitchen. They all looked so different after the makeover and probably would not be recognized so easily.

"Wendy now might be a good time to look for help," Andy suggested.

"Who will help us now?"

"Darling, we still have a magic horn." Zack placed it on the large oak table.

"I suppose it may be helpful. Martha did tell us to use it in case of an emergency."

"This is one of those times. Maybe we can be guided to our next mission," Andy suggested.

"We might even get some good weapons as well," Wendy added.

The three voted to use it right away. It was a critical situation, and it may save them.

# Chapter 7
# The Horn

Like Martha told them, they had to go to the place they landed to access the Portal. They all prayed together to get there safely. They had to do this even though their heads were wanted on a platter.

Hopefully, the new look Wendy gave them would help. Just in case they took several large steak knives, two iron pots, and a couple of baseball bats. It was easy to carry since there were three of them.

They took several deep breaths and left. It was a wonderful day outside with the sunup high, birds singing, squirrels and rabbits running everywhere. It was hard to believe that such a beautiful world had so many hidden dangers, even though the flowers were in full bloom and the sun was shining.

The children had to move smoothly through the streets, and not say hello to anyone. They could not trust one single soul now.

Luckily for them they made it to the spot they landed, but the hard part was to avoid the CORT supermarket nearby. At any moment, a killer could come out.

"I will keep watch," Wendy said.

"I am here for you, darling," Zack said.

Andy was the one to blow the horn. He used to play one back in his school, so it should be an easy task. Hundreds of thoughts raced through his head: Where were his parents, his friends, and Buddy too? He remembered the good times and bad times together. He felt his thoughts swirl like an ice cream cone. He felt lightheaded for a minute and he blew the horn. Its sound created a force field around them. The same moment bullets and darts started flying. They bounced off like marbles and landed outside the force field. The people who attacked them fainted from the harsh force light, their faces turning pale like ghosts.

"Are they dead?" Zack asked.

"I have no idea, but where did that powerful magic come from?" Wendy inquired.

"I think Andy blew the horn just on time."

Inside the shield a timer appeared, set for twenty minutes, and the countdown started.

"We only have twenty," Wendy said.

"I see. Hurry up, little bro!" Zack called out.

Soon, a familiar purple swirl appeared and inside there dressed in purple stood Martha.

"Hello, my beloved children," she greeted.

"Why did you send us to hell?" Wendy asked.

"I am sorry, none of what happened was planned. We have our own major problems back home."

"What is happening?"

"A huge war between dark world and light took place; now we have no resistance or life left."

"You mean all my friends and family are gone?" Wendy asked.

Andy blew the horn; its sound created a force field
around them. At the same moment bullets,
and darts started flying and bounced off.

"Only a small group is left, but we won't last long," Martha finished.

"Oh, my goodness, what is going on?" Zack asked.

"Something in the past has destroyed the future," Martha said.

"Any idea when the drop of Grace started?" Zack asked.

"No, but I think you already know, since you are being hunted by CORT." Martha pointed at the two men on the ground outside the shield.

The timer went down to fifteen minutes.

"We do not have much time!" Zack called out.

"I see, how sad; I have no place to take you," Martha said.

"We must get back to 1992," Andy said.

"It figures, but I have no way of bringing you there."

"We will discover that on our own," Zack said.

"All we ask for is some weapons and our powers back," Wendy pleaded.

"I can get you weapons, but I do not have the power to bring your magic back. That is up to each of you," Martha said.

"Weapons will be just fine," Zack agreed.

"Okay and remember, there is no time or space. Everything is an obstacle blocking your paths," Martha said.

The moment she vanished; they saw three familiar rods in her place. The portal vanished. The shield had five more minutes left on it, and the horn vanished too.

Each child picked up their old weapon. It was the rods that created electricity and had the ability to short-circuit the enemy. The moment the children picked them up, all their cool moves came back to them. They also noticed a new button on their rods.

"Look at this—they have been upgraded," Wendy said with a smile on her face.

"What has been added?" Zack asked.

"It looks like it is a stronger shield with shooting feature," Wendy said.

"So cool!" Andy exclaimed.

"I think we will be able to use it right away," Wendy said.

When the counter hit zero, the protection around them disappeared. When it happened, Wendy pressed the button. Instantly a purple light surrounded them. They moved fast as more people encircled them.

"Put your weapons down," voices called, "you are under arrest."

"Don't think so, man." Andy pressed the other button. Right away the rod opened, and rays of red flew out. They hit the enemy right away, flying through the shield Wendy had on. All twenty men sizzled and fell to the ground. They were unconscious, but still breathing. The children took a moment to run. In fifteen minutes, they made it back home. It was great to feel the protection again. Now they had lots of planning to do. From the wise words Martha told them, they knew that discovering time travel was within reach.

# Chapter 8
# Cracking the Time Code

S itting at the kitchen table, with the ugly wallpaper all around them, the kids began planning.

"What do we do now?" Zack asked.

"We need to crack that code," Andy said.

"That will be a tough task," Wendy admitted.

"Let's start with some plans," Andy said.

"We now have protection, and we have the ability to fight back," Andy said.

"That is a good thing, boy," Wendy said.

"It is a start, darling, but to get our powers back would give us a burst," Zack said.

"Maybe the key is to connect to our inner self," Andy said.

"That might work, little bro."

"It might require meditation we learned with the monks," Andy said.

"It is worth a try. What is the best place in your house to do that?" Wendy asked.

"I have to guess the closer we are to the magic source, the better," Zack stated.

"It will have to be in our basement," Andy replied.

"Great, let's do this," Wendy agreed.

"Let it be," Zack said.

With those words the children went downstairs. Fortunately for them the basement was remodeled into a family area about four years ago. It was here where Buddy, Papa, Mama, and the brothers would gather. The area had a wonderful fireplace, a large couch, and full carpeting. Oh, the books that surrounded them. It always was Andy's favorite place, after his room of course.

This was worth a try and who knew, maybe it would work out for the better.

The three of them sat together on the carpet, cross-legged and silent. The magic glowed around them, their bodies relaxing and radiating light. A strong inner peace took place within. All three kids felt like they were floating on cloud nine. Several brilliant colors and smells and the crackling fire became real. They were not here anymore but in a garden with a waterfall. Was it astral travel or was it more powerful than that? Their whole bodies were refreshed, and they once again found themselves back in Gold Lake. That was the moment that changed everything. This time there was no Martha, but the lake still glowed. A quick jump and a wash and the spark came back once again.

The children woke up all wet and glowing.

"Wow, we did it!" Andy called out with excitement.

"I could not believe it," Wendy said with a smile.

"That was pure genius," Zack said.

"I missed that so much." Andy created a cloud of water around him. Zack got his healing gifts back, and Wendy could once again see the future.

"Now we are ready to face them!" Zack called out.

"Just keep in mind this is a different world and our powers might work differently here," Wendy said.

Andy did not think of that. In here, magic was present; outside, who knew.

"You are right, Wendy," Zack said. "We do not know how our powers will work here."

"That is why we have these," Andy held out his rod.

"Good point, little bro," Zack said.

"At least we know it works," Wendy said.

"All we can do is try our powers outside," Zack suggested.

"Let's use our backyard," Andy said.

"That probably will not work. The magic covers our whole space, including the backyard," Zack said.

"You are probably right, and I have a feeling many enemies are waiting just beyond this magic field," Wendy said.

"With our weapons in hand we might be able to protect ourselves," Zack said.

"We probably have to try out our powers one at a time," Andy said.

"That makes lots of sense; one can cast the shield and one can fight, while the third can practice," Wendy suggested.

The brothers agreed with her.

"Should we do it now?" Andy asked.

"Let's go!" Zack yelled.

Each of the children picked up their weapon and headed out the front door. Wendy put the shield up, and Zack was in front ready to strike. Just to be sure, they only moved away about two hundred feet from the house in case they needed to run.

Just like they expected, many enemies were waiting to take them. There must have been about four dozen.

"Look what we have here," Andy said.

"You test first, we got you covered," Wendy said. The huge shield was out, and gunshots were being reflected. The distant scream of half robots was everywhere. These were no missionaries, but CORT soldiers.

"How did they find us?" Zack asked.

"Someone must have told them," Wendy said.

"Well, anyway, let's do it, friends!" Andy closed his eyes and imagined a huge fireball appearing in his hands. He watched as it grew larger and larger and he launched it toward the enemy. Nothing happened. "Looks like there is no magic here," he called back.

"That really stinks, little bro." The bullets kept flying. The kids could hear them banging hard against the shield.

"Give up, you weaklings," a harsh robotic voice called at them.

"Never, ever, you monster!" Zack jumped several feet from the ground and hit six robots with his weapon.

"Holy cow," Wendy exclaimed. "It looks like you got a new power here!"

"Hell, yeah!" Zack hit six more. The twelve were short-circuited right away.

"That tells me that only physical gifts work here," Wendy said. The shield let out a few sparks, and Wendy noticed she was able to see the movement of each very clearly. It was like time itself slowed down.

"So cool."

"Little bro, you must also have a new gift. Try something physical," Zack said.

Andy stopped making magic and swung his hand a few times. He could barely see it move. "I think I got John's old power."

"Cool, now we know the truth," Zack called back.

"Let's move back to our space now; the shield will not hold much longer," Wendy said.

"Okay," the brothers called back. They dropped the shield and took off. Bullets and sharp objects were flying at them, hitting trees and walls. Robotic war cries were heard, yet in the background birds were singing and they felt peaceful.

They got back home within a few minutes and closed the door behind them.

"I think I have figured out how to crack that time code," Wendy said.

"Please share your idea with us, darling," Zack said.

"I think to crack the time code we must combine our physical powers and meditation magical powers as one."

"How can we do that?"

"We will need to divide in two groups. Andy has

to stay here in the house, and you and I have to be outside the protected area."

"I cannot leave my little brother behind. I made him a promise."

"It is the only way this will work. Andy is no child anymore; you must trust him," Wendy said.

"I will be okay, and we can keep in touch with these." Andy took out three old walkie-talkies.

"I remember these," Zack said.

"Yes, we had great times with them," Andy said.

"Yes, Mom and Dad would carry them too, and we communicated with each other."

"That is correct. We must do this for Buddy, our parents, and the world."

"I guess it is time for me to let you finally grow up, little bro."

"I think I grew up right after I fell through the portal back in the game," Andy said. With those words the brothers hugged and went their separate ways.

# Chapter 9
# Division

It was getting dark fast, but it did feel better being alone. Holding the walkie-talkie in his hand, Andy headed downstairs to the basement. It was scary to be alone and it kind of reminded him of being back in Remake school. Whatever kept him alive? It was luck and hope. He would need that once again.

In five minutes, his machine came alive. First it was buzzing and then followed by Zack's excited voice.

"Little bro, we are in position, and it looks like everything is quiet on the southern front."

"I read you loud and clear, big brother."

"When you are ready say the word," Zack said.

"I will," Andy said.

Five minutes passed and a code was heard on Zack's side—zing, zang, and tick. It was followed by silence.

"That is, it, Wendy," Zack said.

Together they activated their physical gifts. A huge cloud appeared above their heads and they heard a drop. Andy had made it to the spot. Within seconds time around them stood still. Birds did not sing, winds did not blow, and life became frozen. A hand cut through space and instantly a hole appeared in front of them.

"I think we have done it," Andy said.

"Teamwork is great," Zack said.

"We throw a good party," Wendy said.

With those words, the children jumped into the hole. It looked familiar to Andy.

"I think I have been here before," he said.

"I cannot believe that time itself is the dark world," Wendy said.

They walked in single file and could see light coming from them.

"That means we are still alive," Andy said.

"I know, I have heard many things about this place," Wendy said.

"Yes, it really exists. I had to go through here to retrieve one of the items," Andy said.

"I doubt it is at all safe," Zack said.

"A very dangerous place, big bro."

"We must be extra safe." Wendy got her rod ready.

"It did not work too well last time," Andy said.

"Hopefully, we only have to be here a short time."

As those words left Zack's mouth, the children felt like they were floating up. The darkness faded away behind them, and rainbow swirls of purple and green surrounded them. Their bodies felt like feathers, and soon they found themselves on the ground again. The town looked the same but without all the technology.

"Do you think we are back in 1992?" Wendy asked.

"Have no idea, darling, way before my time," Zack said.

"Way before my time too," Andy added.

Wendy forgot for a moment that the brothers were

still kids. After all they went through, they seemed much older.

"It might be best to look at a newspaper," Andy suggested.

"A good idea," Zack said.

The children started looking around them: in garbage bags and on the floor. They saw it. Something that looked like a shooting star flew through the sky and landed three miles away or so.

"That is, it," Wendy said.

"I think you are right," Andy said.

"We are in the right place," Zack said.

# Chapter 10
# CORT Underground

The children started running toward the star. They had a feeling it was Zoey.

"We must hurry," Wendy called as she sprinted forward. She was too fast for the boys.

"Come on, Wendy," Zack exclaimed, "I need to catch my breath."

"There is no time, big bro." Andy ran right past him. Overall, it took them one and a half hours to get to the spot. Our heroes could see the scorched earth in front of them, and whatever the item was, it was gone.

"We were way too slow," Andy said.

"Why did you not use your magic?" Zack asked.

"I tried, but nothing worked."

"Wendy, darling, do you still have your gifts?"

"Nope, not in this world."

Zack tried his gift too, but nothing happened.

"Looks like we were not born yet, our gifts are useless here," Andy said.

Wendy pressed the shield button, and it came up right away. "I think we only have our weapons."

"It is better than nothing," Andy responded.

"Very strange, here only our rods work," Zack said.

"I am worried—how will we get back to our time?" Andy questioned.

"That is something we will need to think about after our journey ends," Zack said.

"I agree, we have much more important matters to fix now," Wendy replied.

Andy looked at the dirty road and noticed a path. "We have something to follow, guys." He pointed to the path.

"Let's follow it," Zack said.

The children walked with a fast pace. Soon they came to a huge wall.

"It has to be our way in," Andy said.

"How could that be?" Zack wondered.

"I suggest we look for hidden doors," Wendy and stepped toward the wall.

Zack knew what Wendy was talking about. It was the same girl who was a leader of a massive resistance. This was the same girl who knew everything about secret doors. Zack did not forget it was Wendy who saved him from flying missiles; most likely if it were not for her, he would have been long dead. "Let's do it!".

With those words the children started tapping the wall. They were looking for something that didn't blend in.

They heard Andy's voice from somewhere.

"I think I have found it."

Zack and Wendy were by his side. They found Andy standing in front of something that looked like a lion's head. They watched Andy as he banged on the lion's head. Soon, they heard a loud cracking noise, and they were looking at a wide-open door leading underground.

It looked like the Remake school, where Andy was humiliated and tortured. It was one huge hallway, but not as high tech as before. There were no isolated rooms for torture; there were no TVs or super advanced computer systems. It reminded the party of a prison. It did have several cells with children in them.

Zack recalled from an article he read, about how a huge increase in child abductions had taken place in the nineties. His mother had told him how she tried so hard to save those poor kids. "Andy, now I know what Mom meant with her stories to us about this time." It was a sad sight to see boys and girls in cages all throughout the gray and black hallway. Surprisingly, green plants were everywhere, giving some hope to our heroes.

"Look at that," Wendy pointed at the blooming plants in the wall cracks.

"How can plants survive in such a dark place?" Andy asked.

"There must be some kind of energy source here," Zack suggested.

"Could it be magic?" Wendy asked.

"No definitely not. I have been trying to do magic, but it doesn't work." Andy said.

"Suppose we are on the lower level, like a dungeon of sorts," Wendy said.

"It is very possible, honey," Zack said.

"I bet it is, since I have seen their cities close many times and they will always have levels," Wendy continued.

**The children started running toward the star.**

"Whatever it is, we will need to let these children out," Andy said.

"It might be better to do that on the way back; it is not like these children could fight. They did not grow up around civil war, magic training, and military arts," Wendy said.

"That is a good point, or maybe in this world they have," Andy added.

"Let's ask." Zack walked over to one of the nearby cells. Inside, he saw a pale boy who was about seven years old. "Do you know how to fight?

All he heard in return were sobs and "I want my mommy; get me out." The cells filled with calls for freedom. There must have been at least three hundred children. Each of them wore one-piece suit with lightning bolts on it.

"This is horrible," Wendy said.

"I think they will be transformed into CORT soldiers," Andy stated.

"Let's risk the escape, boys," Wendy commanded.

"It will be too dangerous, darling," Zack said. "We do not know how far in the process they are." More cries of help filled the room.

"They are just children like us," Andy said.

"I will lead them out," Wendy was determined to help.

"Honey, it is way too risky."

"I think I can take care of myself. We split here. I will meet you in the forest." With those words, Wendy pressed the rod, and blue darts filled the room.

It looked like a huge firework display. Every one of them hit a lock to each cell, with perfect aim.

"How did you do that?" Zack wondered.

"I think I have mastered my weapon finally, been training in private for hours," Wendy confessed. As the cell doors flew open, all three hundred children were free. Wendy was gone, and the two brothers were left alone.

"My love," Zack called out.

"Big bro, we got a mission to do. We will see her soon."

"You are right. Let's go. She is better trained than we are," Zack said with sad eyes.

The brothers took off and passed by the now empty cells. Just in case the shield buttons were pressed. Amazingly, something here made the weapons work stronger, and there was no time limit.

At the end of the hallway, they saw another door with CORT officials guarding it.

"I got this," Andy called out. He pressed the button on his wand, and two beams of light hit the guards. They were caught by surprise. After a few circles they collapsed onto the floor and started sparking.

"Deactivated," Andy confirmed. The brothers ran up the stairs and found themselves on the second floor. Their eyes were wide open with amazement. In front of them were several buildings one after the other. It was like they were back in Old York once again.

"Wow, little bro. Look how advanced they have already gotten."

"I do not get it one bit," Andy said.

"Why would they need Zoey's chip for?"

"I have a feeling it is something beyond a city."

"It has to be. I am worried about Wendy," Zack said.

"You know she could take care of herself. Do not forget she saved us,

"You are right." She will be fine.

The buildings here were also surrounded by several parks and an orange graveled brick path. The boys noticed plants on the street and even a few green houses.

"It looks like they are prepared for a long life here," Zack said.

"Looks like that, big brother."

"We still have a mission; we must find Zoey."

With those words, the boys raised the shields and took off down the path. Our heroes dodged missiles, bullets, and darts. Walls, plants, and trees fell around them.

"Ready, big brother? Let's fight back." Andy pressed another button, and more light strings came off his weapon. After each hit, he could hear a distant sizzling sound. He knew that a robot was down.

The landscape flashed by as they ran. One missile just missed, as the boys jumped behind a red wall. They sat there for a moment catching their breath. Next to them they noticed a familiar face. It was Zoey. She must have gotten away. The kids also noticed a huge hole in her head. It looked like the deactivated chip was just ripped out and she was left there to die.

"Zoey!" Andy tried to shake her awake. It took some time, but eventually her eyes opened.

# Chapter 11
# Zoey Returns

"**W**here am I?"

"Hey, Zoey, what's up?" Zack asked.

"Who the hell are you? My head stings."

"I am Zack. Do you not recognize me?"

"I never met you in my life."

Zack could not understand what was going on here. He remembered meeting her a few times. Maybe she was hit with amnesia or something like that.

Andy stepped forward. "How are you, Zoey?"

"What are you doing here, Sage Andy?"

"Saving another world, I think," Andy said with a smile.

"I cannot believe you let me go," Zoey said.

"I wanted to grab you, but I could not see you."

"Where am I anyway?"

"You are on my planet now."

"Is my world okay?" Zoey asked.

"When I left it was, but things have changed for the worst now."

"What happened?"

"The dark world took over," Andy said.

"Why does my head hurt so much?"

"Your old chip was removed when you were unconscious," Andy said.

"Who took it from me? I will show them!" Zoey raised her hand as if casting a spell.

"Zoey, our powers are useless here," Andy said.

"How could that be? I was so powerful. How can I even survive?"

"It takes time to adjust."

"How did you get so far," Zoey asked, "and who is that clown over there?"

"That is my big brother, Zack."

"Have I met him before?"

"You might have."

"Give me a break, little bro."

"I do not remember him one bit. How come a boy so cool hangs out with that clown?" Zoey asked.

"Come on, Zoey, you have to remember me," Zack pleaded.

"Nope, but it is nice to meet you." Zoey put out her hand.

Zack could not understand how she had forgotten him. He thought back and he technically did not meet her; it was Andy who saved all the sages.

"It is a pleasure," Zack said.

"We have much to do, and very little time," Andy said.

"Will you travel with us Zoey?" Zack asked.

"I can barely move, but I will do my best to help you out," Zoey said.

"Andy are you sure she will be able to make it?"

"I certainly can." Zoey stood up and had to duck again after a few missiles just missed her head.

"Holy moly, are we in the middle of a war zone?"

"What did I tell you, Andy," Zack said.

"Yes, Zoey, I think we activated the alarm." Andy said.

"How do you guys get around here?" Zoey asked.

"These things still seem to work here." Andy showed her the rod.

"They have been upgraded too," Zack added.

"How can our future weapons work so well here? It is very strange. The technology in this world is so old."

"I am still trying to find out how or why," Andy said.

"Do you have an extra gadget for me?" Zoey asked.

"We only got three from Martha," Andy said.

"Martha was here? What did she say?"

"She told us the dark world has taken over," Andy said.

"How could that happen? Everything I loved was back there," Zoey said with tears in her eyes.

"We also lost our family, friends, and dog," Zack added.

"I do not understand how this evil power has taken over," Zoey said.

"All we know is it has something to do with that old chip of yours."

"We must find it right away," Zoey said.

"That is our mission," Andy said.

"Get those shields fired up and let's go," Zoey said with new hope in her voice.

# Chapter 12
# Red Zone

The moment the shields turned on; a strange red light started flashing. A computer voice repeated, "Red alert, guards in place."

"Looks like we have been spotted," Andy said.

"We better move fast." Zoey rushed.

The walls around them started opening, and robots of all shapes and sizes poured out. Some robots looked like humanoids. Other robots were animal like. They all had red lasers shooting out of their mouths and eyes. They seemed very advanced for 1992.

As the party moved, the shields protected them from all kinds of flying objects. There were bullets, bolts, lasers, and even large lights. The party moved fast and had no time to slow down. They tried once and all the shields fell. They were almost hit. Lucky for them Zoey and the boys ducked, but They felt their hair get glazed.

"Zack, I think those weapons are controlled by static energy," Andy suggested.

"If you are right, we cannot stop moving," Zack said.

The moment they got up and started running, the shields worked again. They could hear the walls around them sizzle and spark.

"Wow, those must be powerful weapons!" Andy yelled.

Suddenly everything stopped.

"You think they need to recharge?" Zack asked.

"I do not know, but we should run quicker," Andy suggested.

The party moved faster, and the bullets flew over their heads. Robots chased them. The landscape changed into an underground scene. Gold and black buildings started to appear.

The kids could not believe that they were still underground because they did not see any sign of it. They were running through the city streets and even felt the temperature changes as they ran.

Suddenly, all the weapon flying stopped. They must have been in a residential area. They looked around them and saw people attending their business.

"Wow, what a big change," Zoey said.

"I cannot believe they built so much already," Andy said.

"It is surprising, since we are still in the past," Zack added.

"What do you mean we are in the past?" Zoey asked.

"This era is before our time, Zoey," Andy explained.

"How far back are we?"

"In our timeline it is 1992."

"Yep, we were born much later basically," Zack said.

"Wow, how did I end up so many years back?"

"I think you fell through a time portal in the dark world," Andy said.

"That is sadly true. We also had to travel through there to get here," Zack added.

"Wow, I am like a hundred and twenty years in the past," Zoey said.

"That is about right," Zack said.

"It still amazes me how much they have already finished," Andy repeated.

It was great to be out of the red zone. It was a very scary situation. Just imagine every step you took could kill you. The boys and Zoey were incredibly happy to be in a quiet area.

A familiar scene appeared in front them. They found themselves looking at large TV screens hung on every corner.

"Talk about déjà vu," Andy said.

They saw a large robot face.

"Hello, citizens of CORT underground," a melodic voice called out. "We celebrate today, so let us party." Suddenly music started, and all street activity stopped. People were dancing in the streets.

Everywhere the children looked, people were dancing. Some were doing hip-hop and others the tango. They could not believe their eyes.

"Wow," Andy exclaimed.

Soon the streets were full of dancing people and robots.

"What kind of place is this?" Zack wondered.

"What a strange scene," Zoey said.

"I can't believe that CORT actually used to party," Zack said.

**The Walls around them started opening,
and robots of all shapes and sizes poured out.**

More weird stuff started happening. Various rainbow wildflowers fell from the sky, and food trucks pulled up to one area of the city. The citizens were having a great fun time.

The children watched as the celebration continued. After about thirty minutes the voice came back. "Okay, guys, gals, and robots the party is over Back to work." The music stopped and everything went back to normal.

"That was amazing," Zack said.

"That is something you do not see every day," Andy said.

Zoey stayed quiet and stared into space. Something even stranger happened. The area they were in shifted, and once again the bullets started flying. They were back in the red zone.

"What the hell!" Zoey fell on the ground and watched as bullets just missed her head. The boys pressed the shield button and were once again protected. "Do you think what we just witnessed was real?" she asked.

"I have a feeling it was. CORT playing with our emotions." Andy suggested.

"How do you know that?"

"I was in a Remake school for four or five days."

"I do not remember any of that" Zoey interrupted.

"Well, you were my caretaker of sorts; you went by the name Miss Weed Two," Andy said, looking at Zoey.

"Was I good to you?"

"Nope, not really, but it was before I broke the spell you were under."

"I am sorry for all I did to you, Andy."

"It is okay. You had no control of what you did."

Zoey's eyes filled with tears. "I wonder how many children I hurt."

Zack looked at Andy with wide open eyes; he remembered how he was searching for his brother for such a long time. It probably was the worst experience in his young life.

As the party ran and dodged more bullets, they heard a familiar bark.

Andy looked around and saw someone he recognized. His beautiful dog Buddy was huddled near a wall while his little body was shaking. He seemed to be barking with emotions. As a matter of fact, Andy felt like he was crying.

"Oh, my goodness, Zack, it's Buddy!"

"I must save him!" Andy leaped and grabbed his dog.

# Chapter 13
## Buddy

**B**uddy recognized his owner right away, and before Andy could do anything, his face was full of dog slop.

"I missed you so much; did the bad guys take care of you?"

All he got in return were two happy barks. It was amazing to have one of his family members with him again.

The room shifted again, and they found themselves in a massive forest area. "They are doing it again," Zack said. In the distance they heard a waterfall and a running river. The green was intense, and the air never felt so fresh.

"How are they doing this?"

"I have no idea, Zoey," Andy said.

"We are also lost like you," Zack said.

"I forgot, so sorry. You are also scared," Zoey said.

Suddenly, a huge wave appeared from nowhere, and started rushing toward the party.

"Watch out!" Andy grabbed Buddy and dove for cover; the others followed close behind. They made it just in time. The wave missed them by inches.

"What is going on here?" Zack asked.

"It looks like they are playing mind games with us," Zoey added.

Andy grabbed Buddy and dived for cover;
the others followed close behind.

"If it is mind games, why is everything so real?" Andy asked. Buddy was still in his hands when the room shifted once again. The party had to raise shields because darts, missiles, and bullets started flying again. The children had to move fast. Several more shifts took place. Several scenes flashed as our heroes ran. Fields of wildflowers were followed by cityscapes and eventually by more CORT robots. The party had no time to catch their breath.

They didn't realize how advanced technology was in this place. All they could do was keep moving. They went through bridges, tunnels, and massive cities that seemed to have no end. They had no idea how deep down they were either. They lacked the magic they once had. It was a very tough journey full of surprises and amazing sights and, danger lurked in every corner.

"This place is endless," Andy broke the silence.

"Come on, little bro, we both have been through much worse."

"That is true, Zack, but this journey seems forever."

"I think that we can do it," Zoey pushed.

Two happy barks were heard. Andy looked in Buddy's ear and saw a flashing light.

"I have a feeling I know how to take care of this." Andy smiled. He put his hand into Buddy's ear and pulled out a red bead and smashed it against a wall. The moment he did, all the images vanished, and they finally saw themselves in a huge city—and just at the end of a green path, a tower soared above them.

"Wow, Andy, you did it," Zack said.

"The new sage saves the day," Zoey praised.

"I am sorry, Buddy, Andy said, but I had no choice."

"You just saved Buddy and us," Zack said.

They ran over to the tower. In large letters was written Lust Tower CORT center.

"Like before, they hide in a tower," Zack stated.

"Crazy robots—no offense, Zoey," Andy replied.

"I deserve what you said. I was the one who was controlled."

"Your chip must be in there," Zack said as he pointed toward the tower.

"Let's go!" Andy yelled.

# Chapter 14
# Lust Tower

The group ran as fast as they could toward the front of the tower. When they got there, there were no guards anywhere.

"This is very odd," Andy admitted.

"Let's get the shields up," Zack said.

The boys pressed the buttons at the same time, and once again they were covered.

"What about me?" a familiar voice called.

The boys and Zoey looked up. Wendy was standing in front of them.

"Wow, Wendy, you cleared everyone fast," Andy said.

"There were four levels of cells, and I found a secret pathway out," Wendy said with a smile.

"How far away is this path?"

"It is rather close; it goes deep under the city. It reminded me of an old sewer system."

"I bet this place was built over it."

"In this world levels are used all the time."

"We have subways, pipes, and catacombs," Andy said.

"Andy never forgets cities," Zack added.

It was good to see everyone together again. Wendy raised her rod and opened the shield. Now all of them were protected. They ran toward the door. Surprisingly, they found it wide open.

"I think they are expecting us," Andy guessed.

"I had a feeling they knew the moment we passed the red zone," Zack said.

"Get ready for anything," Zoey said.

The party entered the door and found themselves in a massive tower. The ceiling must have been fifteen feet high.

"I wonder how many floors are here?" Zack questioned.

"We will find out soon enough." Wendy said.

"Do you think our shields will last?" Andy asked.

"I have a feeling we will be good." Wendy's words were confirmed by two loud barks from Buddy.

"Looks like Buddy agrees," Zack said.

"Wow, your dog is very cute," Wendy said.

"I love him very much," Zack said.

"I do all the work," Andy said.

"That is true." Zack smiled.

The group continued to move through the hallways. It was way too quiet for them.

"I bet we will be jumped soon." Zoey said.

"It looks like it is empty," Wendy said.

They continued to navigate through the place. All they saw were endless locked doors. They noticed some scattered plants that found their way here. Some rats and mice passed by. The silence gave them a strange feeling. It was like a huge ghost town.

Shattered glass old newspapers and magazines were under their feet. That familiar smell of tar and old shoes came back again.

"It is like I am back at home," Wendy said.

"I wonder where everyone is," Zack said.

As they went deeper, the place got darker and fewer signs of life appeared.

"Do any of you know where we are going?" Wendy wondered.

Everyone had blank stares; they had forgotten one thing—a map.

The tower was massive and empty.

"What do we do?" Andy asked. He had a great idea; he looked at the others and smiled. "I think Buddy will be able to guide us."

"How would Buddy know?" Zack asked.

"I think your brother has a point; Buddy had to get that chip from somewhere here," Wendy said. It means there is a connection between Buddy and CORT. It is this connection that can guide us.

"It had to be put in him in a computer lab of some kind," Andy said.

Buddy barked twice, and before they knew it, he was off. The others followed close behind him.

"He must have understood you," Zack said as his breath got heavier.

They ran through gray hallways, turned several times, and went up at least twenty levels of stairs. Buddy did not stop for one breath. After about thirty minutes, he led them to a glass room. Andy's idea was good. The party was looking inside a massive computer lab of sorts. The walls were full of glass tanks and behind them were several clones of all different ages and sizes. There were not only people but animals too.

"Oh, my goodness," Zoey said. Zack, Wendy, and Andy stared in amazement.

"Wow, Buddy, you went through so much. I am so sorry." Andy petted Buddy.

Wendy's eyes filled with tears. "This is horrible."

Everyone agreed on this concept.

"Looks like CORT is building a massive army," Andy said. The party also noticed a few cases full of chips. There must have been many thousands of them.

"That must be the brain of the clones," Andy suggested.

"It certainly looks like that," Zack agreed.

"If that is true, considered it destroyed!" Wendy pressed a button on her rod, and thousands of blue bullets flew out. They shattered the cases and destroyed the chips. All they could hear were massive sizzling noises, like a barbecue in mid-August. It turned into a firework show as the chips fell out and shattered. The moment this happened, several blue lights went off. It was when the room started rising.

# Chapter 15
## Rising

"Looks like another moving room," Andy said.

"Here we go again," Zack said.

"I guess the mistakes never stop," Zoey said.

"Keep in mind, this is an older model. We are back in 1992," Wendy explained.

As soon as she said it, several robots appeared around them.

The battle started.

Buddy barked and bit a nearby robot. Right away it short-circuited.

"Look at Buddy go." Andy pushed another robot off the lift.

Nearby, Zoey, Wendy, and Zack were battling.

It was amazing to see Wendy go. The rod moved quickly in her hands. It was like rod-to-robot combat.

"I see you learned some new tricks, darling," Zack called out.

Wendy smiled as she hit another machine. The room went faster.

"Shields up," Wendy called just before they hit the roof.

They got out just in time.

"Wow, what a rush," Andy said. They noticed two locked doors in front of them. "What a strange code." He pointed at the door.

Suddenly, Buddy became jumpy and started barking.

"What is with the excitement about, Buddy?" Andy asked, as he petted the dog.

"I think he knows how to get in," Zoey suggested.

The party watched as Buddy barked happily.

"Do it now," Andy said.

When Andy gave the comment, several barks in code came out of Buddy. As each bark came out, a red light lit up on a door to their right.

"Wow, it is encoded in the dog," Andy said.

"You have a smart dog. Is he really Buddy or a trap?" Wendy questioned.

That question echoed in everyone's ear.

"I know how to tell," Andy said. "Our Buddy has three birthmarks on the right side of his back." He moved his hand over that area softly. "It is he. I have found the marks."

"I have a feeling that chip we removed made him smarter," Zack said.

After five minutes, the door swung open.

They found themselves in a massive ghost room. It looked like an abandoned warehouse.

"I bet it's just another illusion," Wendy said.

"How can we destroy it without magic?" Andy asked.

"I learned something really cool." Wendy took her rod and threw it across the room. The children watched as a blue flame came out of it and smashed in the far wall. The rod was gone, but the whole room changed.

They were standing and staring at a massive computer center. Thousands of machines were blinking, and a massive cool feeling filled the room.

"That is so cool, darling," Zack praised.

"Zack, I thought it over. It will not work out between us."

Zack stared at her with wide-open eyes and tears filled them.

# Chapter 16
## New AI

**E**ven though Zack was hurt, he knew deep inside that it will not work out between them. They were so different and from different time periods. He looked at her quietly and walked away. Out of nowhere a loud voice said, "Looks like little Zack's had his heart broken. Hah."

"Who said that?" Zack called out. The moment he did the whole room filled with romantic pictures depicting Zack's and Wendy's love story.

"Show yourself!" Zack yelled.

"I already have. I am part of you and your brother. It was an experiment that fell apart."

"We are people of flesh and blood!" Andy called out.

"Is that so?" Several more animated pictures appeared all around them—images of the children's births, the school they went to, and much more.

"What are you?" Wendy asked.

"Each of you was a CORT experiment. We tried to make the perfect humans, but it was one big failure. It was you who made this world. Zack, Andy, Wendy, and Zoey, all this is your fault."

Several more pictures appeared all around them. Images of everything they had done to this point. All their adventures rolled up in a perfect little ball.

As the red shield became brighter,
and stronger each person connected.
It was then a yellow glow surrounded them.

"What are you?" Zoey demanded.

"I am you and you are me," the voice said with a dark laugh.

"This AI is more advanced than the other, we destroyed." Andy said.

"Did you really destroy me, or did you create me?" the voice said.

How did a machine know so much about them? How could a machine be so powerful?

"I will show you something." Andy pressed a button on his rod, and it emitted red ray.

"Do you really think a tiny weapon like that can destroy me?" the voice called. The shot bounced back at him, turning his rod into ash. As the dust fell from his hand, a powerful shock hit his arm.

"Look who is fried now."

Andy looked at his hand. It was black for a moment and healed. He had never seen anything like this; his magic was still present… "I need to connect. Protect me, Zack." His brother was the last one with the weapon in his hand.

"Got your back, little bro." Zack activated the shield. It surrounded them all. Zack released his anger, and the shield became bright red. It glowed like a fireball. "Your magic is still here; you just have to access it again." Zoey closed her eyes and connected to her inner self through emotions of love. As the red shield became brighter and stronger, each person connected. A yellow glow surrounded them. They were one team; they were soul mates. Each of them gave a puzzled look toward the building. The moment the yellow glow appeared; a strong rush of power filled each of them. It was everything together: the family and friends they loved, the adventures they had, and the bond they shared.

The burst of magic filled their bodies, and the shield vanished in a pop of smoke.

"I feel good!" Andy called out. He felt that power once again and he started chanting something. Lightning bolts appeared in his hands, and he shot them randomly into the room.

"You think it will be that easy? You are wrong, boy," the voice yelled. Those words were followed by red flashes, then glass filled the room.

# Chapter 17
## Glass

The lightning bounced off the wall and started flying everywhere. The party had to duck down.

"Your magic is useless here," the deep voice said. Several doors opened and rolling robots poured out. "Why don't you play with my pets for a while?"

"We must have a better plan," Zack suggested as he smashed a few robots to dust.

"Do any of you have a glass destroyer spell?" Wendy hit a robot across the room.

"I need to think…" Andy kicked a small robot, smashing it against the wall. "Behind you!" he yelled at Zoey.

"Thanks, kid!" Zoey raised her hand out and caught one bot in it. She threw it across the room, knocking out ten robots. "Yes, strike," Zoey yelled as she jumped in the air.

While his friends were fighting all around him, Andy thought over all his spells in his head. There had to be one that could destroy the glass.

"Hurry up, little bro, our time is limited," Zack said.

"I am processing; give me a moment." Spells were running through his head. "I think I got it. Cover me!"

Zack activated his shield. "Got you, bro."

Andy chanted some ancient words; they just came

to him from somewhere. It was a spell he had never heard of. When he finished his chant, the whole room moved. It was like an indoor earthquake.

"What is that?" the computer asked.

Moments later the floor below them opened and swallowed the group. As they fell, they saw things flash in front of them. Their whole history rolled up in one.

"What did you do, Andy?" Zack asked.

"Honestly, I have no idea; the words just came to me, and I repeated them."

"Do you know where the words came from?" Wendy asked.

"Nope, no clue," Andy said.

"I think it is the end of us," Zack said.

"I believe in the young sage," Zoey stated.

The fall began to slow down. The party landed without any pain.

They found themselves in front of the huge red door engraved with CORT TV.

"What does that mean?" Zack tried to push the door open, but it was sealed shut.

"I got this." Andy chanted the knock spell. It came back to him naturally. It was hard to believe he still remembered it. As his chants vanished, the red door swung open. They found it; now it was time to save the world.

# Chapter 18
## Saving

The gang entered a massive room; it looked like an empty ballroom. There was a large oak table, all kinds of plants, and several paintings of CORT founders.

"This is very strange," Zack said.

"I bet it is all illusions," Andy said.

Wendy tapped the table lightly, and a knock echoed back. "It looks pretty solid to me."

Andy closed his eyes and imagined things vanishing. He remembered the time when he and his brother built forts out of tables, chairs, and blankets. He tried hard to recreate the world he loved. He felt a powerful jolt go through his body, and the huge table turned into a massive fort.

"What did you do, little bro?" Zack asked.

"I tried to remove the illusion, but it did not work."

"Does magic work here?" Zoey asked.

"I guess it does since Andy transformed the table into something," Wendy said.

"That is something we used to build as children," Zack said.

"I think it is very cool, but it does nothing for us," Wendy interrupted.

"Andy, harder," Zack encouraged.

"I can't; something is blocking my magic."

Zack spotted it under his brother's feet—a glowing circle. "Can you move?" he asked, concerned.

"No, all my muscles are frozen," Andy said, with fear in his voice.

Before they knew it, none of the party could move.

"It was a trap!" Wendy called.

They heard a voice: "Look what the winds blew in."

The curtains in the corner opened, and a man walked in. He had a huge plug in his head and was wearing all black.

"Who are you?" Zoey asked.

"I cannot believe you do not remember me, Miss Weed2," the man replied.

"I have not been called that in a long time. Which are you?"

"Oh, I know everything about you guys. This time you will not destroy my plans."

"I know who you are," Andy called out.

"The young sage remembers. No surprise for me," the man said in a deep voice with a smile on his face.

"You are SAM," Andy said.

"That is correct, boy."

"We destroyed you in the future," Zoey said.

"Maybe that was the past, not future."

"What are you talking about?"

"You people are so clueless."

"Where are we anyway?" Zack asked.

"No, you are my slaves, and I can do anything I want with you." SAM pressed a red button, and the floor below the party opened up and they fell in.

The curtains in the corner opened up
and a man walked in. He had a huge plug
in his head and was wearing all black.

Thirty seconds later, they found themselves in a massive dungeon. The clothing they were wearing was torn and tattered. Surprisingly, none of them got injured.

"What happened?" Zack asked.

"Looks like our journey is over," Zoey stated.

"I think it has just started," Andy said.

"Do you have a plan, kid?" Wendy asked.

"Not yet, but I will soon."

"Make it quick, little bro," Zack said.

Andy looked around the cell they were in. In one area there was a huge hole, most likely used for human waste. On the other side of the room were two bunk beds and mirrors all around them. "This looks very familiar."

Zoey gave him a strange look. "How many times do I have to say I am sorry.

"Now stop remembering things and blow this place to hell," Wendy said.

Andy took three deep breaths and pictured a wall of fire consuming the bars. Nothing changed. He tried to remember the knock spell and still nothing happened. "Magic is useless here," he admitted again.

"How about plan B." Wendy pointed at the hole in the floor.

"You want us to go through a waste zone?" Zack asked.

"Do you have a better idea? Make it quick, because here they come," Wendy pointed toward four robot guards heading toward them.

"I got it," Andy said.

"What is your plan?" Zack asked.

"We fight them."

"With what?" Zoey asked.

"The mirrors." Andy took the ladder from the bunk bed and smashed in the glass. He picked up a huge piece ready to strike.

"You are a genius, young sage," Zoey said. Soon each person had a large piece of glass.

Soon the robots approached the cell.

"Now is time for your reboot," a robot said. He opened the cell and entered.

"I would rather die!" Andy jumped up and smashed the glass on the robot's head. It instantly fell to the floor exploding. "Mayday, mayday," it repeated as it died.

"Your life is over." Zoey threw a large piece of glass into another robot's eyes. The moment it hit, the robot smashed into a wall and was out.

Wendy and Zack attacked together and took down the last two. The cell door remained open and soon the gang was out.

"You did well, Andy," Wendy said.

"We watch every step," Andy instructed.

The party moved through the underground. On the way they passed by cells holding people.

"We must help them out," Wendy said.

"How can we do that?" Andy wondered.

"Try your magic," Zack suggested.

Andy closed his eyes and pictured a huge knock

spell and remembered how much he loved his family. Buddy was still with them. When the images faded, every cell in the place flew open.

"We must hurry!" Wendy rushed. She still had those leadership skills. It was something that both Andy and Zack respected about her.

People were standing outside their cells waving to the heroes. Andy and Zack spotted two familiar faces in the crowd.

# Chapter 19
## Parents Found

"**M**om, Dad, what are you doing here?" Andy asked.

There was no answer; all the parents did was stare at the boys. Something strange was about them, they looked like zombies.

"What have they done to you?" Zack questioned.

Suddenly, the boys' dad started talking in SAM's voice. "Now let the fun begin."

As soon as those words were heard, a side door nearby opened.

"What now?" Zoey asked.

"We must join our powers together," Andy suggested.

"How do we do that?" Wendy asked.

"Grab on," Andy called out. The group held hands, and a burst of power went through them.

"What is going on?" Wendy asked as her body got hotter.

"This is human power," Andy said.

The room started shaking, and a large spark of pink energy tore through.

"Are we doing that?" Zack asked.

The room moved faster, and the walls flew open. It caused air to enter the cave. The temperature quickly dropped all around them. Yet, the party only felt hot.

The cold air froze all the robots that were about to attack. As the gang held tighter, the room got colder. Everything was freezing all around them. They heard computer chips hitting the floor, and witnessed robots turning into statues.

The others joined hands, and the walls disappeared. They saw it in front of them: a huge computer system.

All the lights were flashing, and SAM's voice was becoming distant.

"What have you done" were the last words everyone heard. Within minutes everything robotic turned to ice. Human connection won. The last beeps faded and what was once CORT Central, became an empty ice cave.

"Andy, what did you do?" Zack asked.

"I did nothing. We all saved the world." Andy pointed at each individual human being around him. As the last beeps and robots vanished, the people finally became free.

The family was united for the first time in a while. Hugs and kisses were exchanged around them.

"Zack and Andy, how you grew up," said Mom.

"I am very proud of you guys," Dad said.

A loud noise came from somewhere.

Everyone looked up at a familiar purple portal. It appeared right in front of them. Martha, Kevin, Ellen, and David came out.

"Meet Mom and Dad," Andy said.

The parents looked up at the strange people in front of them. Each of the sages was wearing a different color robe.

"Your boys have saved us all," Martha said.

"Peace has come back to our world," David confirmed.

"We are getting rid of the leftover CORT soldiers now," Ellen said.

The parents looked proudly at Andy and Zack; they were not boys anymore, but men. That pride was strong. So, all they did was stare in silence.

"Wendy, will you stay or go?" Martha asked.

"I have decided to go back home," Wendy replied.

"Will we see each other again?" Zack inquired.

"I think we must live our lives now; I still have much to learn," Wendy said.

"Thank you for all you did," Martha said. The boys hugged and kissed Wendy and Zoey. They knew deep inside they had to let them go.

"How will we get back home?" Andy wondered.

"We will drop you off," Martha said.

With those words Andy, Zack, Buddy, Wendy, the sages, and the parents entered the portal. After rainbow swirling colors and purple flashes of light, they were back in Trinity, New York, again.

# Chapter 20
# Rebuilding

**W**endy and the sages landed in the middle of Icy City. It looked vastly different than she remembered it. There was no ice anywhere; lush gardens were scattered all over town, and buildings were starting to be rebuilt again.

Something seemed hugely different for Wendy. There were no statues honoring her resistance. Everything told stories of the sages only. No Zack, Andy, John, or Wendy had even been mentioned. It was like they never existed.

"What is the meaning of this?" Wendy asked.

"What do you mean, Wendy?" Martha looked at her with concern in her eyes.

"Those boys and the resistance saved this world twice, and they have been erased from history."

Martha looked at the other sages "Who is she talking about?"

"I am talking about Zack, Andy, and John."

"You just dropped them off," Wendy stated.

"I think this girl is a bit confused. Go home, dear, and sleep," Martha said.

With those words the sages vanished.

Wendy did not understand what was going on here. She thought she came home to a peaceful world, but it looked like history had been changed and the memories of the sages had been wiped out. They seemed to remember her, but not what she or the others did. There were many questions Wendy had to find out for herself. She was happy to come home to her house, and it was great to see her family again. It was like she had never left and never had any adventures.

"Wendy, dear, how was your school?" her mom asked.

Wendy looked at her and smiled. "It was fine." As she went to sleep, she knew there still was a huge mystery to solve. Was the civil war truly over? Was it just the beginning of something much bigger? As she fell asleep in her bed, Wendy had much on her mind. She would never give up until the mystery was solved and the adventures, she had with her friends would never be forgotten.

There was no ice anywhere, lush green gardens were scattered all over town and buildings were starting to rebuild again.

# Chapter 21
# Happiness

**Z**ack and Andy were happy to get back home and find their family. When they got home, things haven't changed. The supermarket was once again out of business; the train station they were on before was gone. They also found out that the library and New York City was back too normal.

"What is going on?" Zack asked.

"It is very strange," Andy added.

They found a pile of homework to be done. Summer was finishing up and school would be starting again in a few weeks. Little League was over, and no more missing posters were found. It was like the boys never left Trinity. Could their whole adventure for many days be lost? Deep inside they missed Wendy, John, and all their friends, even though everything seemed to be back too normal and they would be children once again. They had two weeks to catch up on all the summer work they missed. They still wondered if the adventure was finished or just beginning. They also thought about everything they had left behind. Was this truly happiness?

The answers were deep inside their hearts. They did not know if they had changed history and if all they had accomplished would be lost.

# Acknowledgments

I would first want to thank my parents and my sister for all the support that they have given me as I worked on this book. I want to express my gratitude to my wonderful team of people at Outskirts press bringing my vision of "Rebirth" to life. I especially want to thank my mom for her wonderful editing job.

Thanks to Michele Sobel Spirn for all her mentoring and guidance she gave me as I was working on all three books. I also want to thank Victor for all his wonderful illustration that brought "Rebirth" to life. Thank you to all my local businesses in my wonderful neighborhood of White Plains, New York and in New York City for letting me spend hours putting my trilogy together in the early years of my books.

# Illustrations